The Doll

written by **NHUNG N. TRAN-DAVIES**

illustrated by **RAVY PUTH**

Second Story Press

Long ago, in a nearby land, there was a young girl
whose eyes were deep-ocean blue,
whose dimples twinkled like bright mischievous stars.

She was waiting.

To and fro, her skinny legs dangled from a plastic chair,
as planes landed and lifted above cotton-candy clouds.

In her hands, she held a small doll,
with wild curls of cinnamon, lips sweet and rosy.

"When will they get here, Mama?" the girl whispered.

As the words rolled off her tongue, the metal gates slid softly open, and the back-and-forth pacing of adults stopped.

A hush washed over the waiting people.

Through the gates
they came.

Five, six, seven...
a mother and six children
in ragged clothes,
clutching a tattered bag.

Holding all they had left.

Forced from their home
by the cruelty of war,
down to the shore they'd
fled to cross unfriendly seas,
risking hunger, cold, and even
death for a chance at life.

Boat People, they were called.

With hesitant steps the family shuffled forward.

On eager feet the crowd surged forth with open arms.

From behind her mother's legs, a child timidly peeked with eyes round and brown as chestnuts, hair as black as night.

Her lips quivered, and her knees trembled.

Then all was still.

Into her hands, the young girl placed the doll with curls cinnamon and wild, lips sweet and rosy.

On the child's tanned face,
a smile cracked open
as radiant as a ray
of new hope.

A little scar on her cheek
dimpled with mischief.

Her eyes shone like stars
as she cradled the doll.

She had traveled far,
suffered much,
and had so little.

Words were not spoken.

But this one act of kindness
said that she was welcome.

It told her she was home.

The child slept safely
clutching the doll that night
and for many nights
that followed.

And as she grew taller and stronger,
she dared to dream.

The girl studied hard and worked harder.

She became a woman. She became a doctor.

She could ease the suffering of young and old, here and there.

But always, always she kept the doll with her.

Then one night, news images flickered on her television set.

Scenes of people fleeing, like her, a long-ago Boat Person.

People with nowhere left and nothing to bring, desperate and scared.

Children and families in search of hope.

The young woman reflected on her own journey over unfriendly seas.

The doll stared down at her from a shelf.

It seemed to say,
"All that you have,
and all that you
have become
are because of
an act of kindness.
A moment in time."

At an airport, metal gates
slide softly open.

A young woman waits,
as planes lift and land.

Then, four, five, six...
a mother with five children
in raggedy clothes.

A colored hijab on her head,
all they have left in her hand.

With hesitant steps the family
shuffles forward.

On eager feet, people move
with open arms.

From behind her mother's legs, a child timidly peeks,
eyes round and green as emeralds, hair shiny as light.

Her lips quiver, and her knees tremble.

Then all is still.

Into her hands a young woman with midnight hair
places a doll with wispy curls and rose-sweet lips.

On the child's timid face, a smile cracks open.

As radiant as the morning sun.

A little scar dimples on the woman's cheek,
with a playful mischief long gone missing.

A small act of kindness from a long-ago
moment is not forgotten.

It ripples outward, beyond our doors,
over our steps, across the seas,
and welcomes weary travelers home.

AUTHOR'S NOTE

When I was a little girl back in the 1970s, there was a war in the country where I lived, Vietnam, which is in Asia. Nearly a million people had to escape, mostly crossing the sea in crowded boats. We suffered sickness, hunger, and some boats were attacked by robbers.

In 1978, my family—me, my mom, and my five brothers and sisters—were some of these "boat people." Along with 300 others, we crammed into a rickety fishing boat and set out across the ocean in a storm. I was four years old then, and the waves were so high. I was very afraid.

Luckily, we made it across the sea to Malaysia, where we spent eight long months in a refugee camp. Helpers from the charity Red Cross gave us food, and we climbed a nearby mountain for wood for fires and to build shelters. Then we got the news that the people of Our Lady of Mercy Church in Enoch, Alberta, Canada would welcome us to their town.

When I walked through the gates of Edmonton International Airport, a beautiful girl named Adrienne was waiting for me with a doll. Her gift made me feel really welcome.

Forty years later, now a grown-up doctor, I saw the stories on TV about the war in Syria, which is in the Middle East on the Mediterranean Sea. I wanted to do something to help another child whose life had been turned upside down by war. It was my turn to stand in the airport and welcome six-year-old Alma with a doll.

Nhung's doll, on display at the Canadian Museum of Immigration, Pier 21, Halifax.

For Adrienne, whose kindness and compassion forever changed my life.
KMS, may you remain humble, grateful and resilient.
—Nhung N. Tran-Davies

To Menda, Avan, Mom, Dad and my large family.
To all the refugees in the world that have left their home under unimaginable
circumstances: your path may be complicated, but know that you are an
inspiration, especially to people you have never met and maybe never will.
Thank you.
—Ravy Puth

LIBRARY AND ARCHIVES CANADA CATALOGUING IN PUBLICATION

Title: The doll / written by Nhung N. Tran-Davies ; illustrated by Ravy Puth.
Names: Tran-Davies, Nhung N., author. | Puth, Ravy, 1987- illustrator.
Identifiers: Canadiana 20200333240 | ISBN 9781772601657 (hardcover)
Classification: LCC PS8639.R38 D65 2021 | DDC jC813/.6—dc23

Text copyright © 2021 by Nhung N. Tran-Davies
Illustrations copyright © 2021 by Ravy Puth

Edited by Kathryn Cole

Printed and bound in China

Second Story Press gratefully acknowledges the support of the Ontario Arts Council,
the Ontario Media Development Corporation, and the Canada Council for the Arts for
our publishing program. We acknowledge the financial support of the Government of
Canada through the Canada Book Fund.

 ONTARIO ARTS COUNCIL
CONSEIL DES ARTS DE L'ONTARIO
an Ontario government agency
un organisme du gouvernement de l'Ontario

 Canada Council   Conseil des arts
for the Arts   du Canada

Funded by the Government of Canada
Financé par le gouvernement du Canada |  Canada

Published by
Second Story Press
20 Maud Street, Suite 401
Toronto, ON
M5V 2M5
www.secondstorypress.ca